PETER AND THE MAGICAL POT

PART 1

MANORAMA JYOTSHNA SREEMANTHULA

ISBN 979-8-89363-956-8

Contents

1

The Pot

It was the year 1999, a pot has been created to shield their world and send it far away so that when the time comes the pot will come back to help them. The speed with which the pot is coming down is trillion times to that of the speed of light. It was supposed to be land on Saturn but it was asteroid struck so it started coming towards a beautiful planet, Earth. The pot landed on earth but don't know where and there were rumors that a UFO came to the earth and took someone. Next day there was a complaint that a boy called Sam, 12 years old went missing and no one knows how did that happened.

Another incident happened in the same city in the year 2009 and again no one knows why did that happened. This time no one was missing but the whole city along with the neighboring cities lost power of lights, cars, phones, torches. Even match sticks are not burning. This was the time when our beast got its super powers. It was lying on one of the tables of Museum of National History and they labeled it as THE POT.

It was the time of sunset and in the museum cameras won't work properly for three seconds due to glare. Our little beast slept for long and it started opening its eyes one after the other and waiting for the sunset by rubbing its down part on the table with hee hee sound. It cannot speak but still makes sound. By the time the clock strike 6, the pot split into two and one remained there and other with lightning speed went to all the night guards and dropped pot bomb on them. They fell asleep. It goes out of the museum with small rumbling sound drunnnnn…..drunnn…drunnn.. drunn….. drunnn… and eats up all the food lie in the closed shops nearby and also goes to nearby sea and collects stones and shells. Thus the life of our beast is going very happily until our hero enters its life.

The Museum is nearly 2000 years old and due to heavy storms and raining it was demolished. Now the pot is very sad and don't know where to go. Just then a bunch of people came to the Museum and started collecting few things. They took the pot to very big place with many steps in it and there is a board "THE AUCTION".

2

The Auction

350 Million dollars - first time! 350 Million dollars - Second time! Three fifty million dollars- third time! It's really good to hear that sound on the phone and I almost felt like I'm winning. Finally I'm at the auction.

Peter Bright Intro

Hi! My name is Peter Bright. I'm a Successful business person at the age of 9 years. I don't have my parents and don't want to know about them because business people only focus on the future.

Hobbies: Only losers have Hobbies

You can find me: Only at Auctions and Betting Spots cause I'm busy.

Profession: Born with Business Spoon so obviously a successful Business Magnet.

Assistants: Maya and Kaya.

According to my assistants Report the evolving Current Flame On me is The Cruel, Victor. Last time I won 750 million dollar worth portrait in the auction over him. We are the two forwards who always bid for a place in the world. He hates me and I hate him. Both of us square our hate from both sides.

Scene 1: Peter entered inside from the door.

Ahead, the enemy was already visible. Peter began to study the surrounding, "I thought I was running behind the schedule but made it on the count!. The reality is kind of fishy here. He is not active in the auction and just leaning in the chair. That's odd. I believe he is afraid of me. No, I don't think. He is always unafraid of me. Then what is it?"

Just then, "Wait!" Peter raised his voice against the auctioneer, "I bid for that portrait and you are selling this scrap to me." He pointed his finger towards THE POT and his face was red. The vibrations of the word 'scrap' extended till the beast and now it is extremely in a mood to hit him.

He then notices a cruel smiling face appearing him. "Finally, I won the portrait", Said the voice. "Let me guess, you are working for a portrait that has already been sold out?" asked the voice. It was Peter's treasured antagonist, Victor. Peter experienced a cruel disappointment. $350 million is nothing to him but the key point here is about the prestige. He is angry with the pot and also don't want to take it but he anyway should sign the papers.

Announcement has been made. Victor and Peter have been coming opposite to each other on the ramp to get to the auctioneer. The mischief of the Victor, however, was not ended.

Victor Self Intro

I'm Victor. I'm the most handsome bachelor with bunch of girlfriends already. People never regret talking to me. I'm a down-to-earth Person. Media People always envy my Status that's why they always paint Not-So-Nice Picture of my behavior.

Profession: MD of "The Makers" Studio

Enemies: Peter Bright, My sworn enemy

Hobbies: Auctions, Photography and eating Cupcakes

Assistants: Lily and Jane

Scene 2

As Victor and Peter were sharing the ramp to get to the auctioneer, they had noticed something before them. It was an old brown colored raised on the ramp side and is about 20 feet height by 10 feet width followed by small key pockets at different stages.

It was written 'Charity Benefits the Giver more than the Receiver'.

Peter looked at Maya and Kaya who always carry hearing ears (Bluetooth) as one of their body parts. Maya started saying "Mr.Bright, People are always afraid of going near it.Once money goes into that box it belongs to the charity. It's an Ancient box which is opened for every 25 years. It's been 15 years for now. The main chamber has 12 small chambers and the eighth chamber is cursed and no one ever opened that chamber.

Last time Miss.Cecilia accidentally lost her auction cheque that fell into the box.

"Miss Cecilia! She is the MD of this auction right?" Peter asked.

"You are right as always Mr.Bright" said Maya and Kaya.

The walk got finished. They are now near the auctioneer to sign the papers. The beast is now getting a greater chance to have a closer look on Peter. The pot is superbly self-respected so it won't tolerate people disrespecting it but it never respects others in return. During its stay in the museum it has learnt so many things not from the museum books but from the night guards mobile. 'Michael Jackson -Beat it....' And Brittney spears – 'toxic' songs are its favorite hobbies. Peter and Victor gave their signatures. All clapped.

The boys were crossing themselves from the auction segment to the audience then a terrible thing happened that left everyone speechless. All of them rose up at a time. As the best enemies were coming downstairs, Victor consciously tripped Peter so that he can take the advantage of his fall but even Victor got horrified with what he has done and to escape the fighting he fled from there.

During his trip Peter lost his bracelet with a key into one of the key pockets of that charity chamber. There were many tubes connected to the key pockets. The bracelet was moved fast from up to down hitting different places and it went into other tube. All the people are watching whether it falls into eighth chamber or not. Finally it was supposed to fall into eighth but suddenly fell in seventh one. Everyone got upset little as they were expecting eighth chamber.

They heard a whistle sound which is made out of happiness and no one knows from where did that sound came. It is the whistle of the happiest one who is none other than The POT. The Ego of the pot is little satisfied with this incident.

Everyone was staring at Peter as if they expected him to faint or something. All knew that the bracelet is Peter's entire property. Even his house also opens with that key only. Peter got on his feet and started to put his hand in the key pocket to remove that bracelet.

Just then a voice said, "STOP". Peter thought it would happen and he knew her coming.

Cecilia is a fair girl with very long caramel hair and dressed the best. Her face is very attractive that anyone would fall for her but none of them have the courage to face her.

Cecilia faces towards the audience and says "This property belongs to the charity and no one should touch it. According to my knowledge auction has been completed 15 minutes before itself." She started looking at the watch. All of them except Peter and Cecilia at once emptied the room.

Cecilia said, "I'm sorry I cannot help. Rules are rules for anyone."

Peter didn't say a word, lost in his own thoughts and started leaving the auction.

Cecilia Self Intro

My Heart Belong to: Auctions, I am the Prime mover, the maker and of course the only Breaker of this Auction.

You can find me: With my Red diary

If that's not the case then: Cuddling with my Pets

Love: I love attention

Things I Hate: I really hate funny and dirty people

Life Ambition: Want the most Precious thing to sell for a world record price in the auction.

3

Peter's Journey from Mr. Bright to Mr. Dim

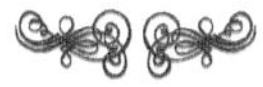

Peter started walking out of the door with an empty mind. He doesn't know how to react for his situation. He is neither sad nor angry. It was raining heavily and he sat on a stone nearby hugging himself. He was soaking wet and was shivering like a leaf.

It's been two hours but no one came for him. Now he is realizing how people around him change and how rude he is been with other people and his employees who are nice to him. He understood that it's waste of time going to his house (means his Ex-house).

By the time the clock strike twelve he saw a shadow shining in the rain and is appearing towards him. He turned back but was not able look properly because of rain. The figure started staring at him with sparkling big eyes and smiling face and came so much close to him as if to kiss him.

Peter calmly stood up with his shivering body and gently asked "who are you?"

There was a boy standing in front of Peter smiling. He is similar to that of Peter's height, medium toned and has dark berry eyes with curling hair. He has a plastic cover on his body to protect from the rain and he removed it. Now the boy's body is also upset with rain. His clothes are looking like rags and one of his shirt shoulders was torn.

"My name is Thomas" he said smiling and covered Peter's shivering body with the plastic cover he was wearing before.

"I came here for you Mr. B……." the boy was still saying. Peter stepped forward and hugged him close. There were tears in Peter's eyes. He swiped his tears and finished hugging.

He was not able to say 'thank you' to Thomas because saying 'thank you' was just not enough Peter thought to himself. Thomas held the hand of Peter and they started walking. Peter never felt this much safe with someone before. He always used to doubt people.

Peter saw Thomas and couldn't understand how Thomas was able to smile in such a critical situation. It was raining so much and he was shivering but his smile didn't change a bit. The rain got slowed down and it's just sprinkling now.

Peter said "I think it's a long journey".

"It's just three lanes away" replied Thomas. "You didn't ask me where we are going. Mr.Bright"

"Because I don't have any choice and don't call me Mr. Bright call me Peter. You are my friend right" Peter said.

Thomas jumped out with excitement and making his eyes big he asked, "You are my friend! Really?"

"Yes" Peter said. Thomas face was glowing like gold in the sunlight. Peter and Thomas smiled at each other and started for their destiny.

It's like they have experienced all the seasons at once in this day. It started with raining then went cold and the hotness just passed ten minutes before now it's like spring. Their togetherness ignored all the things happening in their surroundings.

Finally Peter and Thomas reached a place. Peter looked up and it was written "GO ILL" on the board.

4

The Orphanage

The Board is really weird with that name and the gates are rusted and one of gates is sleeping on the floor. The house was looking like someone cleaned it after so many years. There was mud water everywhere and it was flowing through the gate.

Peter soon realized that it's not a house but an orphanage by seeing group of children who is gazing at him in amazement from the windows. He was in dilemma that why the name "GO ILL"?

Thomas who noticed Peter which he always do started saying, "It's a 'GOOD WILL' foundation". Peter started laughing hearing this.

"Where do the other letters go?" Peter asked.

"Two owls always come and take them away" Thomas replied "It has happened several times."

They both started to proceed inwards.

Thomas took Peter from backside as if he is hiding something from someone. They just then hit with a very large round ball shaped creature.

She was a woman and was dressed like a nurse. She opened her mouth and started using all the special words on Thomas for an hour. With the speed she was shouting it almost cleaned the floor dust and she pointed her index finger on Thomas and left.

Thomas bent checking if she left or not.Then he told Peter, "We use this technique every day to clean our dormitories"

Peter couldn't stop laughing and said, "I didn't know about this technique otherwise I would have applied in my home." While talking they reached a place where many beds are placed in a row. It's a very big hall and there were array of beds arranged there. The inside of the orphanage was very neat when compared to that of outside.

Thomas and Peter sat on a bed and Thomas said, "She is Aunt Lora head of boy's dormitories and Uncle John is the head of girl's dormitories"

While Thomas was speaking something strike Peter in his mind. "How do you know that I was sitting at auction in rain?" Peter was eager to know the answer.

"I actually don't know" Thomas said. "A rich looking boy in the car told me when I was at the signal".

"Your Peter Bright has become Peter Dim", this is what that boy said and vanished into the road after the signal was green. "I know that today is auction day that's why I came there directly."

Peter was puzzled and asked "How does he look like and how do you know me?"

Thomas, "Are you kidding me! You are one who used to donate toys for us." And then said " I don't know. I don't remember him properly as he is sitting in the car but he has yellowish hair and cylindrical faced."

Peter then remembered that the toys he used to throw as waste were given to this people. Peter was thinking that the boy who told about him must be Victor because Victor is cylindrical faced and has yellowish white hair and he is rich. But how did Victor know about Thomas and why did he tell Thomas about Peter. Peter got confused and was about to ask Thomas but they are continuously hearing hiss... hiss... sound from wall side. Thomas asked Peter excuse and went out.

There were children standing like a grape bunch from top stairs to down. They made a cue to meet Peter Bright.

"How does he look like?" one boy asked.

"Does he look like same in TV?" The other boy asked.

"Is his teeth real or fixed one?" another boy asked. All of them surrounded Thomas so much that he is not able to breath. They started holding his hands and squeezing them with their doubts. Thomas became restless.

Thomas said, " hussssh... slow down you guys." But no one is ready to slow down. "Yeah.. Yeah.. He looks like same in TV. His face is fair and diamond shaped and he has black eyes and black hair." Said Thomas.

Peter sat there for few minutes and felt something is wrong and went for Thomas. Thomas was facing other boys and speaking to them. Peter appeared from back and said "Hi". All the children opened their mouths with amazement and fell one on another. They started surrounding Peter and now he is not able to move.

Just then a voice shouted, "Stop!"

She is a fat beautiful girl about a height of Thomas with chubby cheeks, rosy fair and curly hair. She was carrying a shiny old golden color basket with a lid on it. She smiled and told everyone to leave that place and they can meet Peter in the evening. All of them left at once. Her voice is really mesmeric.

She turned towards Thomas and smiled. They both smiled at each other and all the three started walking into the room. While walking Thomas said "Peter her name is Clovey and she brings cupcakes to our orphanage". Peter and Clovey saw each other and smiled. They all sat on the bed.

"Peter, are you hungry?" asked Thomas.

"I could eat something" said Peter.

They ate the cupcakes brought by her.

5

Peter Bright and Kevin ADAMs

It was evening and the view was really nice from outside. Peter never saw this side of the city. The orphanage is the last house from where there is the beginning of darkest forest. He is enjoying the view. Just then Thomas appeared with a jug of

Then he gave autographs to all the kids with his signature.

A boy of six to seven years came to Thomas running. He is a small boy with cute face and was holding a Rubik's cube which was half solved. He told peter "door-someone".

Peter and Thomas went out.

There was a boy standing outside with formal garments with gloves to his hand and an envelope. He is Very good looking than any other boy they have seen before. His face is shining with the brightness. Thomas mouth was wide open till they reach him.

"I think I have seen you somewhere" Peter said.

He said "yes, I'm Kevin ADAMs, the new partner of the Auction"

Thomas intervened "so you came to give his property back?"

Kevin growled and said "no." He turned towards Peter and stated that "There is still chance you can get your previous life. But there are some conditions."

Thomas "why are doing this and how are you related to this?"

Kevin " my father is a partner with Cecelia and there is a flaw in the document that if instead of money any item falls into it so then half treasure is given back to them"

"So what are the conditions?" asked Peter

"First you have to prepare a document to claim your property and second is......." Kevin Paused

"Second is….?" Thomas was curious to know.

"Second is, you need to keep the Pot with you and after 14 years the chamber will be opened. Till then you have to keep this pot safe."

Peter was in dilemma because he is happy here than before and he hates that pot. He was about to say no.

"Ok, not a problem" Thomas said keeping his hand on his beloved friend's shoulder.

Kevin smiled slightly and said "Thank You". "Come to my office tomorrow in the evening at 6 and I will retrieve your pot."

Thomas intervenes "can I come with Peter?"

Kevin says "sure, why not. Our office is so big that your whole orphanage can fit in it."

Peter "Why don't you come in and have a cup of tea?"

Kevin "may be some other time". He handed address card to peter. The card was slightly big than normal cards and there was auction house picture at the top and followed by name "KEVIN ADAMs".

Peter and Thomas bid good bye to Kevin and his car left

Thomas starts to go inside from tomato plant side but Peter stops him by keeping his hand in front of Thomas.

Thomas looks at peter and Peter was staring at him crossing his arms with an eyebrow raised.

Thomas says, "What?????? I'm not jealous of you people."

Then Peter asks "why are you jealous?"

Thomas says, "I'm not jealous because I'm not worried."

Peter asks, "Why are you worried?

"I'm not worried because I don't think you people will become best friends." Thomas says with doubted face.

Peter laughs and says, "No, I already have a best friend and no one replaces him"

They both smiled at each other and went inside.

6

Victor's Entry

It was quarter to eight in the night, Thomas and Peter got their dinner after standing in the cue for half an hour from downstairs because it was Sunday. On Sunday there will be a large variety of dishes available. Most important among them was Clovey Cupcakes. Noby readily arranged the bed for all them to sit and eat.

When returned back to their place, Thomas and Peter saw something which was beyond their imagination. There was a tall person with yellowish hair, graphite like coat and a denim trouser giving a rich look to his personality. Peter and Thomas looked at each other as if they knew that person even though they saw him for the first time.

"He must be that Chicken heads father" said Thomas while they are walking towards that gentleman.

"Good Morning Mr.Bright" He said with a sorry tone "I wish I would have known what happened in auction before"

"Good Morning Mr. Opher", Peter said and was about to express his words just then the Cruel enters the hall.

Victor said with cruel smile, "Its ok dad. People get what they deserve."

Mr. Christopher said "You are absolutely right son. People get what they deserve".

Victor and Thomas were shocked to hear this while Peter understood what he is saying.

Thomas got very angry at Junior Opher and Senior Opher and was ready to give blows but Peter stopped him. Victor looks at Thomas from top to bottom and changes his face expression as if he ate bucket of tamarind at a time and says "Looks like Peter Bright got new friends here"

"Ok then Mr.Bright it's great to meet you and now I take permission to leave" Mr. Christopher smiled. Thomas and Victor were confused about why he came without any purpose.

In front they were able to see a big size figure coming towards them. There comes Miss. Lora with an envelope in her hand which she handed it to Mr. Christopher. He handed that letter to Victor.

Victor mind read the letter and he was face was red like blood, "I remember you saying that we are going to vacation father" he screamed.

"This is your vacation son. As a good citizen it is your responsibility to take part in the sorrow of your friend and also after seeing the CCTV footage of the Auction I made my mind clear that Peter tripped because of you."

Thomas took the letter and read out.

From

Victor Opher

Dear Peter,

I am sorry for the great loss you are facing and I'm ashamed being a part of it. Being a friend and citizen of this city I take the responsibility to the mistake I have committed.

I am Mr. Victor so far have decided not to go back to my place taking an oath to stay with you as long as your property won't return. Here I took the admission in your orphanage and coming to you.

Yours Lovingly

Opher.

There was an admission letter attached to it.

Thomas face was smiling when he finished reading the letter but Peter was sorry for Victor.

Victor angrily went downstairs and stood near the bushes while Christopher was talking to Peter that he can take responsibility of all expenses of Peter or else can come to his home but he knew that Peter would deny and which Peter eventually did.

Down Victor who was so much angry started scolding Peter and to his surprise he was able to hear someone scolding him the same words back. He looked around but no one was there. Now he got horrified. One side of the bushes with a green chili plant started moving and the other side remained calm.

Everything went normal after few seconds and Victor again started scolding Peter. Now there was a little flying sound Victor can hear near to his ear. He turned back and saw that the green chili are started to convert into red one by one and are flying.

One red chili with a crown on his head and stick in his hand started examining Victor and after few seconds of examination he whistles twice and all the chili flies attack him and vanish.

Victor was burning heavily but there were no marks on his body. He started screaming loud with his crow like voice. All the People rushed down and picked Victor up. He went near Christopher and started saying that he saw red color chilies and they bite him.

Christopher laughed loudly and said "I told you Thomas, didn't I? My son always makes this kind of pranks. So please ignore them". He left the place leaving Victor behind.

Everyone ignored Victor and left to the hall. Victor got so much terrified that he ran back of them.

7

The ADAMS Office

Victor was still angry but he had no choice other than obeying Thomas. The hall was fully packed.

Thomas says, "Here hold this blanket and sleep with Noby"

Victor saw Noby and his bed was not looking good.

"I will sleep on this bed" Victor pointed his finger towards his beside bed.

"No. That is Peter's bed and no one sleeps on his bed" said Thomas.

They both started to argue but Peter agrees Victor to sleep on his bed. Thomas didn't want Peter to share his bed with Victor so he said Peter to sleep beside Noby. All agreed.

All started sleeping and lights were off. Victor first somewhat struggled to sleep but later he got into deep sleep which ultimately made all other children to wake up.

First he started snoring slowing then it was so much huge that it can be heard down. Thomas couldn't sleep a wink. Every time he starts to doze off the snoring would start again. Victor on other hand slept like a panda.

It was Monday morning; everyone is having breakfast downstairs in the lawn. There were many long wooden tables arranged. There were several bowls which were made out of wood. Everything which is in the orphanage's limit is mostly made of wood. Victor joined Peter and Thomas.

Did you sleep well?" Peter asked Victor.

"It's impossible to sleep in a place like this", he said with a strong voice, "I have my own designer room in my home and I won't allow anyone to sleep in my room." He added.

"No one will dare to come to sleep with you I guess" Thomas said in a criticizing way.

"Yes" Answered Victor proudly.

All the people started laughing at this and Victor didn't understand because he didn't about his snoring last night.

All the children heard a huge bell and stood at once. Peter and Victor were confused and they stood as well. Then there were a group of children who were marching with baskets in their back. Few were carrying in their hands with wood and honey. All stop at once after entering inside and Noby from the last came front with a list in his hand and started guiding children where to place things.

Peter and Victor were amazed to see Noby leading a team.

"Is he the same boy from yesterday?" Victor asked Thomas with excitement and surprise.

"Noby is very good at remembering the routes and he exactly knows where finds what if he sees it even once. He even discovers new routes in the forest. We have been successful in finding food and wood from the forest", said Thomas decreasing Victor's excitement.

Peter with few other children started cleaning the wood, Thomas was extracting honey out of honeycomb, Victor was busy in counting the bundles and Noby is making sure that everything is arranged properly or not.

All the work got finished. Thomas bought a three bottle of honey and poured to all but Victor ignored to have it. Thomas winked at other children. Few people held Victor's hands and few his legs and made him to sleep on the floor. Thomas came fast and poured honey in his mouth.

Victor liked the taste of it. He got up and drank remaining half bottle. Everyone laughed. Later all of them had a bath at once with water pipe removing all the dirt from the body.

Finally the time came when Peter and Thomas were supposed to go to Kevin's place. They reached the office and waited for ten minutes. Thomas who likes art work started admiring the office art. At the back of them there was an art of a tree with many leaves on a wall.

"This art looks vibrant" said Thomas.

"Every art looks vibrant to you" said Peter smiling without looking back.

"No. This art is the best among all arts I have ever seen" claimed Thomas.

Peter was about to turn back Kevin calls both of them into the room. He greets them and they together have a cup of coffee. Kevin coughed so many times and tells that he is not feeling well from few minutes before. He goes near the chest and opens it.

Thomas cannot believe his eyes. This is the first time he saw a chest which is full of diamonds and gold and also there was a black rusty thing in the between. He thought it must be the post and it is of course the pot.

Kevin takes out the pot and hands it over to Peter.

Peter was feeling strange. "It was looking little big than before" said Peter.

Kevin and Thomas laughed. "You saw it only once so you are confused" said Kevin. Thomas also agreed with Kevin.

Kevin, Peter and Thomas came out of the main room talking and bid good bye. Peter was feeling so strange and was moving fast out of the hall. Thomas on other hand turned back to admire the beautiful art once again but to his surprise there were few leaves missing in the tree.

"Where are the other leaves?" Thomas shouted loud with a surprise tone.

Kevin laughed and said "I guess both of you friends ate something strange". He was coughing hard. Thomas told him to take rest and left the place.

He went outside and saw Peter. Peter was struggling to hold the pot.

"What happened?" Thomas asked.

"It is so heavy", said Peter.

Thomas took the pot from Peter. He looked strangely at Peter and told him that it was lighter than air. Later Thomas assumed that Peter hates to carry the pot that's why he did this.

Peter felt that there is something wrong with the pot. He looked at the pot which Thomas was carrying and it winked at him. Peter got horrified but didn't tell Thomas about it.

Peter after reaching orphanage tied several ropes to the pot and kept it in a bag with password and kept it in a locker.

All the children are leaving for dinner but Victor got a call from his dad and he is answering it.

"Where is it?" Christopher asked seriously.

"It is here. He kept it locked with password." Said Victor with a low tone

"Take the pot and come back home soon." saying this Christopher cut the call.

8

A Night like A Morning

Peter fell into a deep sleep that would last one hundred years. He was sleeping, sleeping and sleeping. Then there is a great *hubbub* in the hall and it is even more deafening than usual. Peter slowly woke up with the blanket rubbing his eyes and is left wondering what all this is about. The clock just strike 11 at night and it was looking like a Christmas Morning.

The *hubbub* was so intense that it would be impossible to hold any private conversation. Slowly half of the noise started leaving the room and it died down few minutes before 12. Every one's attire was looking similarly other than fat and thin issues.

There was a boy standing still near the mirror, running his hand through his hair on and on. It was Thomas.

"Hello Rock star, Night and shine boy" saying this he stole the blanket from Peter and kept it in the cabinet that doesn't have a closet. By the time the clock strikes twelve Thomas hold Peter's hand and hurried downstairs.

Peter asked "what's happening?" He is indeed shocked to see a very large double deck bus with children in that saying 'come fast Thomas or else you will be late'.

"Late for what?" asked Peter.

Peter is now worried about what is happening. Thomas and Peter started running towards the bus. Thomas held Peters hand and was running so fast. Peter was amazed by Thomas speed. He never saw him with that speed. Peter and Thomas were at edge and almost felt like they have lost it.

A boy with Rubik helped them to get in.

"Thanks Noby" Thomas said

Noby smiled, "Ch..Chi..Chik..Chicken He.. Head.. has already got into the bus" he said.

Peter and Thomas have no choice but to stand near the steps foot boarding because there was no place inside. Just then Noby called Peter and Thomas to the upper deck freeing two seats for them.

Victor who had been already enjoying the view saw Peter and Thomas coming. Victor and Thomas opposite to each other near the window and Noby sat beside Thomas.

The double deck bus is very old and painted with vibrant red. Peter was so much surprised with the chandelier that bus has. It was a very old one without rust on it.

"So where are we going?" asked Peter who is sitting beside Victor.

"What is your opinion about Trade?" asked Thomas leaving Peter's question behind.

"Buying and selling of goods" Peter quoted nicely. Thomas looked at Victor. "Earning Profits for ourselves leaving losses to others" quoted Victor.

"What if you don't have money?" Thomas asked counter quoting to both of them.

"Barter" said Peter "We are going to do barter job?"

"S.. Sc..Sch.." Noby is trying to say something. Peter and Victor are looking at his mouth eagerly. "Schoo..School" said Noby.

"The Night school" added Thomas.

"A night school for ten years children on Trading that too barter?" questioned Victor. It was **something** even Peter had never heard.

"Eight y.ye..years…" said Noby smiling and was holding a some pamphlet in his hand. He scrambled his Rubik and started solving it.

"Talent has no limits" answered Thomas.

"But we have no admission, no uniform, no books and no money, no entry pass?" Peter and Victor added.

"Don't worry you don't need money, uniform, admission and books for it" Thomas said.

Thomas and Peter looked at each other terrified and said "Entry pass!" Noby then handed pamphlets to Peter and Victor. They are not pamphlets actually.

"Entry passes" said Thomas laughing.

All the children got busy talking among themselves. Soon they have crossed an old bei

"So how does the school looks like" asked Peter.

"Who knows" said Thomas.

"You people didn't go to the school?" Victor raised his voice a little.

Thomas and Noby looked at each other and they nodded their head. Thomas explained that they went to demo classes only one week before and the school is starting now but they also claim that being native people they heard many things about this school which will amaze all. While they were still continuing their talk the bus got stopped suddenly.

9

The Hermes School

All the children gathered at windows, they moved the red curtains aside and started gazing the outside of the window. The school was 100 meters away from the gate and was huge in size but old. There are so many symmetric patterns seen on the walls of the school. There were symbols of golden baskets with fruits in it, Merchants exchanging one pot with other and so many.

When the children got down the bus and started walking they have noticed that they are not the only children who are attending. There are thousands of children who already been there from different schools and orphanages.

"Now what?" questioned Victor.

"Now get your passes ready", Thomas replied.

Peter started looking around and was thinking something.

"What happened?" asked Thomas.

"I have noticed that there is not a single girl from nowhere", Peter replied.

"It was from the time of gods that this school is dedicated to traders who are men. So no girl is allowed to write the entrance exam." Thomas calmly replied.

"Do we have to write an exam to get into it?" Victor jumped with surprise and said "If that is the case then I don't want to write the exam."

Thomas said, "Go ahead your wish"

Victor rushed back to the bus and was about to enter it. Two boys who are stout brought Victor back holding him two sides to the place. All started laughing. Thomas informed victor that no one is allowed to go back without writing exam. All heard a bell rang and they started running towards the school.

Finally all the gang reached the school. At the top of the school there was a sculpture of a god holding light in one hand and with a golden basket with lots of pots filled with gold in it on other hand. Below there was a carving which is giving a bright shine in the moon light and it was written as "THE HERMES"

Peter and Victor after gazing the sculpture for few minutes started staring at Thomas and he shrugged his shoulders as if he does not know anything about it. Noby was about to say something but the bell rung again so everyone started to hurry. In this stampede the friends chain (Peter, Victor, Noby and Thomas) was broken and they were scattered. Noby fell down and was not able to get up and Peter who saw Noby from a distance reached him with great effort and helped him to get up. So they couldn't make it for the exam. Victor who even didn't make it was waiting at the other side of Peter and Noby having no clue about his friends.

Soon all the people gathered in the room and many people were left outside because no place is left inside. Thomas who already reached inside thought his friends would be somewhere and prepared for the exam.

"Are you ok?" Peter asked Noby, nodded his head but one of his legs and hands got scratched.

Peter told Noby not to go anywhere but to stay where they are now and went looking for the first-aid box. There he luckily finds a safety person who gave some bandages, cleanser and some pills to Peter. He ran to Noby and treated him with the medicine and water.

Peter and Noby sat on a small rock assuming that Victor and Thomas will finish the exam and come. Noby was feeling bad that Peter missed his exam because of him but Peter replies with calm and peace that he is not at all interested in the exam and just came to accompany his friends. Noby heart got lighted after listening to the Rock star.

It's almost end of the exam, Noby thought to himself by looking at his watch. He was thirsty again and also not able to stop walk properly so he requested Peter to bring some water.

Peter told Noby that it is not that necessary to write the exam and they can leave now to Orphanage but Noby who is very passionate and dreaming about this exam from 6 months disagreed with Peter. Peter who already expected Noby's answer suggested him to stay close to the exam gate so that they could cross it before any does.

Saying this Peter went to the same safety place to get water. He drank some water and returned with bottle. When returned he noticed that the door got already opened and all the boys are rushing inside and he noticed Victor at the end. By the time he reached the place it was full and they mentioned that it is the last sitting.

Nearly 15-20 boys were left outside this time along with Peter and the one who wrote the exam came out from the other door and within few seconds the ground was clear leaving only few people.

Thomas who didn't knew the situation came to Peter who was standing near the closed exam hall gate and asked about the exam. Peter narrated the whole story to him and also how passionate Noby is. Thomas felt sorry for Peter. All the remaining boys who were not able to enter inside the hall lost hope and left the place slowly leaving Thomas and Peter behind.

Peter and Thomas who were standing straight in front of the gate and talking surprised to see the hall gate opened just two minutes before the exam.

A senior boy came with the lightning speed and asked, "One seat left. Can anyone join?"

Hearing this Thomas face started glowing like a 1000 watts bulb. Without letting Peter to decide any he took Peter hand and gave to senior boy. The senior boy grabbed Peter hand tightly as if he is a culprit and went inside with the speed he came.

By the time Peter reached the hall all the children occupied the space and the senior boy arranged the way for Peter by making all the boys move aside and pointed a place in the front row. Peter started observing the surroundings like as usual.

The hall was very big and empty with several doors at sides which remained closed as they walked by and there were many floors on it.

Soon the halls were crowded and there was lot of noise going inside the room. Just then all heard a huge clapping sound from upstairs and clapping is an echo of someone. A tall person started coming down and he wore a black suit and a hat without which his face can be seen clearly. He stood at a dark place where the speaker has been placed and there was someone with the same attire accompanying him but no one can clearly see them.

The tall person raised his hand up and there was clapping sound again. Peter and Victor were very much confused about what is happening around. Just then to their surprise everyone sat down at once leaving a little space between each other and before.

Seeing this happen Victor also sat down and Peter is staring at the tall man in the shadow not bothering about what is happening in the surrounding. Victor continuously told him to sit but he is not listening to anyone. Then there was a sudden clanking sound which made Peter to come out of the dream. All the students looked at the doors which were opened at once and a group of hooks with papers and ink in a cover started railing automatically towards the students.

Each student picks their paper and ink from the cover and puts the entry pass which has their name on inside the cover. Peter fills it after picking a paper and ink for him. After trollies left the place, curtains start to fall surrounding single individual as a barrier. When Peter was about to sit he noticed that there were some blood stains and far away there were four to five small leaves.

Victor who is already inside before Peter signs Peter that Noby is the one who got injured. Peter and Victor knew that something was wrong but can't leave the exam in the middle. It's a rule that no one leaves the exam hall before the bell until and unless it's an emergency.

Just then a maid comes and informs "The boy is just fainted no need to worry and if anyone know this boy they can meet after the exam in the nursing room." They were relaxed after listening to the maid.

The exam went for an about three hours which included Topics like Trade, Presence of Mind, Quality, Quantity and of course the best weapon of all humor related questions.

Since Peter and Victor are from business background it was not a big problem for them. All finished the exam and were escorted out. Peter and Victor shouted "THOMAS". Thomas came inside and saw Peter and Victor running so he ran back of him.

"Do you think he is ok?" Victor asked Thomas.

"I wish he is", said Thomas.

By the time they reached Noby lied on bed and they went near him with terrible faces.

Noby is speaking something slowly "I want fruit cupcakes clovey...fruit cupcakes"

"He is alright" said Thomas and Peter smiling.

Noby woke up after few seconds and the safety man gave him some potion for the second time and it was quiet a relief for him and all left for orphanage.

Noby explains in the orphanage that suddenly how his mind got blank and he fainted. He rang the bell beside him which was kept to inform in case of any need for water or emergency.

"I'm sorry. I took your place" said Peter.

"No. No. Don't be. I'm happy for..you..",Said Noby.

Meanwhile Victor comes with two or three branded sunglasses and tries to open the box in which the pot stayed. "Peter, why did you lock this thing?"

"Umm, nothing", tells Peter while opening the box and keeps the pot in his pocket. Victor keeps his sunglasses in it.

"When will be the results by the way?" added Victor joining Peter and Noby.

"After a week" said a voice from the back. It was Thomas.

"Where did you go?" Peter and Victor asked.

"You went..near..my..my.." Noby was stammering. Peter and Victor are curiously watching Noby's mouth that what is he going say.

"Yes" said Thomas. Then there comes a cute looking fat girl.

"What happened to my brother?" saying this, she goes hurriedly to her brother and holds him.

"Clovey is your sister?" asks Peter. Clovey, Noby and Thomas nod their heads. Victor on other hand was very much surprised to see a simple, calm and beautiful girl. He was speechless.

"Everyone had dinner?" asked clovey.

"Yes. We were full", said Victor proudly.

"Even I ate more today" said Thomas. Peter and Noby kept their silence because they know what is going to happen next.

"Oh!" said Clovey.

"I bought cupcakes. I know you people are full but if you want you can have" she showed her towards the golden basket.

Victor and Thomas ran towards the basket and started eating the cupcakes as if they didn't eat anything from ages. Thomas stopped after a while but Victor who ate Clovey's cupcakes for the first time has become mad and didn't stop eating. Thomas forcibly made Victor to stop so that Noby can have remaining 3 cupcakes.

Clovey talked to her brother and insisted him to come to home but he didn't accept.

"You know what he said, don't you?" said Noby in a disappointed tone. Thomas, Peter and Victor sat few yards away from them. "I will try to convince him", said Clovey in a slow tone. Noby nodded his head again.

All the three monkeys are eagerly listening to the conversation and the best monkey who cannot hide his curiosity gets up and starts to move towards Clovey and Noby. Peter and Thomas hold Victor tightly and Thomas tells him, "It's not manners to involve in others personal matters."

"But I don't have manners" Victor says proudly.

"I know that but Clovey has and if she gets angry then no more cupcakes?" said Thomas.

"No more cupcakes?" Victor asked shockingly.

"No more" said Thomas proudly.

"Oh" saying this Victor quietly sat on bed. At present anything which is important to him is cupcakes not Orphanage, not his father and also not his mission.

"I think you should.. g..go..now" said Noby.

Clovey nodded her head and walked few steps with Thomas talking something personal.

Victor who was standing beside Noby was curious to know but worried about cupcakes. He tried to ask Noby once or twice but reminded Cupcakes and stopped. Noby fell into deep sleep.

Clovey bid good bye to Thomas and Victor and left the place.

10

Hoodie Attack on Peter

As Clovey comes down she sees Peter and smiles.

"Thomas told me to leave you till the bus stop" said Peter in a calm voice.

"Thank you Mr.Bright but I don't want to trouble you and I know this place very well", says Clovey with her sweet voice.

"Call me Peter and it's not trouble to go for a little walk with a friend" says Peter

Clovey and Peter smile at each other and leave for bus stop.

Victor who comes to know that Peter is going out tells Thomas that he would accompany Peter so that Thomas can take care of Noby. Thomas agrees.

Peter and Clovey reached the bus stop and Clovey took the bus saying bye to Peter.

Peter who is coming back hit something and fell on it near the street light. It was looking like branch of some tree Peter thought to himself. It was hard and black in color. He dusted off himself and when he saw there was nothing. He felt it was hallucination.

He started walking in dilemma and heard some noise and turned his head back while walking. He hit something again and fell down. It was the same branch again. It was neither a coincidence nor a hallucination Peter thought to himself and started walking fast.

The branches started taking human forms. They were almost ten of them, wearing hoodies started following Peter. Peter started running fast in the other direction of the orphanage.

Peter notices that no one is able to see them other than him. While running there he ...

He reaches the signal and a truck was about to hit him. Someone drags him hard back. Peter becomes unconscious.

 PETER AND THE MAGICAL POT

11

Pot Shocks Peter

Peter was continuously dreaming about the Hermes School and the person in the shadow and the hoodies and he grew quite restless till midnight and slowly went into deep sleep.

When he woke up in the morning, it was eleven thirty and he was almost alone in the room except few notes on his lamp side.

The first note says: "Good Morning Rock star,"

Seeing this line peter smiles and thinks it is Thomas. He opens the note and starts reading what is written.

"I'm going in search of a new job. I took extra bread slides for you and hid it down my bed. Today breakfast was less. Please adjust with it for now."

The second note says: "Sorry Peter"

"Must be Noby" says Peter to himself and reads the note:

"I am going into forest. I'm good now. You are not there for breakfast so I saved you a glass of milk under my bed."

When Peter tries to open the last note which is obviously written by the monkey king, the note smells complete perfume of GUCCI GUILTY BLACK POUR.

"It's good you woke up. I'm not able to find my FENDI sunglasses.

By the way I'm going to meet a friend of mine so I will meet you at dinner."

Peter who slowly getting up to fresh and finish up the breakfast grins at Victor's note. Later he hunts for FENDI sunglasses of Victor with a bread in his hand but couldn't catch it at anyplace. Peter then curves down into a hefty wooden box attached to his bed where all the Victor's clothes are reserved.

He then overhears a sudden thud sound but there was nothing when he turned back. He started looking back into the wooden box yet again overhears a box scraping sound. He speedily turns and to his surprise the pot box laid four to five foot away from him.

Peter was certain that somebody had been playing with him as nobody until he found the truth.

This time he bents so deep to check into the wooden box and something comes and hits him on his butt so he falls inside the wooden box. Peter gets up noticing that there is nothing. He then slowly moves towards the small wooden box trying to open it with a terrified face and finds the glasses there.

Peter with the glasses started moving towards the Victor suitcase.

"I think something is behind me what should I do" he thought to himself. He turned with a horrible face and finds pot flying in air. It ran out running outside and Peter missed it and it ran out of the window.

12

Peter Goes to Kevin's place

Peter was in a foul mood and not able to understand what to do. He thought of going to Kevin's place and to tell him about it. He took the visiting card which Kevin has given him and left for him.

Meanwhile Noby comes from the forest at five and finds none of their friends but only notes. He searches for Peter but couldn't find him and he waits for some time.

It was six by the time Peter reached the office and he directly rushed into Kevin's cabin without listening to anyone. Just then an assistant comes and informs Peter that Kevin did not return from the tour.

She tells him to write a note and put it in the emergency box. Peter did so and left the place.

By the time Peter reached the orphanage he saw everyone was waiting for him at the floor. He thought that the beast had come back and done something. He cleaned all his sweat and tension and went calmly inside.

"Where did you go without informing me?" asked Thomas with anger and concern. Victor and Noby looked at each other face and then Thomas face. All laughed at Thomas who reacted as a concerned mother.

Peter was about to tell but Thomas stopped him and said, "You can talk about it later but first have dinner; these two horses here were dying with hunger." Thomas showed his hands towards Victor and Noby. Peter understood that no one knows about the pot.

13

The Boy Entry

All finished the dinner and sat in the lawn for some time.

Noby sighs something to Thomas who sat beside Peter. Thomas tells everyone to take rest and tonight would be a great night.

"What is so special about it?" asked Peter in a general way.

All are first shocked then remembered that Peter was not present at that time. Thomas shakes Peter hand on behalf of selecting in the admission test. Thomas said that nearly 20 members of the orphanage got selected in the admission test which included Victor, Thomas and Peter. All were happy that together they can go to school. Side walking along the lawn they went to the hall to sleep while Peter who was still in dilemma was the last one to enter the hall. As soon as he entered he noticed that the pot was right there before him.

All start to act like they are sleeping then Noby tossed and whispered "Pete.., are you soaking in the sleep?"

"No" the reply came from other side, "I'm all dried up"

"Even I'm not getting the sleep" said Thomas sitting up straight. Within a few seconds they came to knew that the whole room was awake. They turned on the lights. The boys who were going to school started helping themselves while boys who are not going are helping the boys who are going to school.

"Even a dead man would wake up for this noise" said Thomas excitedly packing his things.

Noby smiled and showed Victor. Thomas concluded that he comes under chicken category. Victor suddenly wakes up giving goose bumps to three of their friends and started searching every nook and corner of the bed. On asking he replied that he heard something like chicken. He gets cool down when Thomas reminds him that according to orphanage rules no one is supposed to bring or eat Non-vegetarian in the orphanage. He also replies that's the reason they rely on the forest for food. It took half an hour to convince Victor about it. Victor who is childish and stubborn won't change his decision once he is decided. It's because of his friends he changed his mind a little.

Peter who was in dilemma whether to take the beast with him or not finally decided to let it stay at the orphanage as no one would come to the hall in the morning. Peter thought deeply and remembered every moment of the pot and noticed that pot is so much concerned about its plate.

Thomas called out Peter as they were going down, Peter sighed them that he will meet them down. He went to the box slowly and saw a sleeping beast after opening the box. Peter hands were shivering, the only thought that driving him right now was what if it wakes up. He felt that his heart would break up into thousands of pieces. Sweat started running down to his chin from forehead in the form of water droplets.

By the second Peter took the plate, the beast opened its eyes and was very angry with the rock star. With a furious face, needle like teeth and strong movement of its eyes was making Peter's body to move but his mind was not co-operating him. It started throwing the things one after the other on Peter. The war went for some time. Peter who realized that its waste of time fighting with the beast stood firm in front of the beast holding the plate.

The beast who noticed the plate in his hand started searching its head plate with its hands. Not knowing what to do it made a crying face while sleeping on the floor. It then started crying loudly which made Peter's ears deaf. Peter soon put it in the box and locked it with two locks and also even locked the hall.

Peter who took all of his body and pot plate to downstairs had rushed into the empty bus silently. He sat in the last seat near the steps holding his breath tight. Suddenly someone put hand on his shoulder from the back. Peter jumped out of the seat thinking that the pot has come out. It was Thomas and on asking Peter told that he was not feeling well after the attack.

The bus got filled like as usual with the other orphanage students joining them. Peter who was sitting near the window opened the curtains while thinking not to tell that issue to Thomas, who already had enough trouble because of him.

While Peter was lost in thoughts and starting at the road saw something went with a lightning speed at the other side of the road.

After observing keenly Peter understood that it was none other than the pot. The pot slowed down and turned his head towards Peter laughing mischievously. It didn't notice its back and got hit by a lorry. Peter closed his eyes when he saw this accident happened and felt sorry for the pot.

He heard someone whistled and looked out of the window. To his surprise the beast was now at the back of their bus covering the distance between them. The whole bus got covered with the curtains and all the students are busy in watching the movie. The only thing Peter was afraid was what if the bus driver watches him. He slowly stood up to get to the bus driver but the beast made its hand as sharp needle and cut the back tire.

With the speed the pot cut the tire made the whole bus to fell down tripping thrice on the bridge. Peter who stood to get to driver was hanging at the edge and Thomas held his hand strongly followed by Victor. All together dragged Peter into the bus and everyone got outside of the bus.

Peter got down gathering all his courage and told it to go back otherwise he would throw the pot plate into the water. The pot got was very much afraid about the plate. It stood still and was not leaving the place. Thomas started calling out Peter. Peter who was in hurry came to pot slowly warning it to not do any stupid things in the school to which the pot has agreed by shaking its body. Peter tied a strip to pot eyes when kept in the pocket and the plate was hidden in the secret pocket of his.

Thomas and Victor who got down later joined Peter enquiring about tire puncture. Peter told that it may be because of some stone and went forward to check the driver. No one had ever seen the driver driving as there was a door between the driver and students. Peter peeped into the driver place through the window but he didn't see any.

All got into the next bus and prayed to the god that nothing has happened to anyone. Peter who was curious to know about the driver went into the cabin and noticed that it was auto driving and there was a camera at the top. Finally the bus reached the destination.

The Hermes was very vibrant to look at. The lawn was full of trees on both the sides and it was looking as if it was a bright day. All the students who cleared the test reached the hall. At first there was an introduction speech given by the school head Sebastian. He face is little serious and he wore a brown vest mixed with white pant.

"Good Morning Gentlemen,

I heard our school has tripped and as School head it is my responsibility......" It went on for a fifteen minutes. Then the wise head Johnson proceeded. He looked neat, tidy and top of the all he voice is quite appealing. He continued over for more minutes and then comes the person for whom Peter was waiting for.

The Head chairman just stood at the second floor while all others are standing at the first floor and no one is able to see him in the dark other than his shadow. Then comes a supporter of him and only a shadow of him can be seen. Thomas and Victor stood side by side with Peter in the middle. Thomas told Peter that the second person looks like a boy. Peter and Victor agreed to him but this second person didn't come the last time they added. Both the boy and the head person wore the hat and were very thin. The head person who didn't spoke a thing raised his hand up and the celebrations have started.

The head boy Sebastian ordered Johnson to show around while he gathered other few people who looked rich. One of the person from that group asked Peter and Victor to join them but they refused to leave Thomas behind. Moreover they were really fond of Johnson.

There are many sculptures arranged in series one by one and the heads started explaining one by one. They were drinks and cakes in everyone's hand. Victor who can't bare his hunger grabbed three cakes for him.

The pot which was no more able to hide its hunger started jumping in Peter's pocket and got succeeded in removing the strip from its eyes. Peter who understood the pot intentions started giving the pieces of his cake. It ate almost eight large cake pieces. Victor was very much surprised to see Peter eating.

"Are you ok?" asked Victor.

Peter replied that he was ok and was very hungry. Victor admitted that he didn't eat anything properly from two days that may be the reason.

Finally they reached the last statue where it was written "Only a KHUNKAAR can break it."

On asking Johnson, he gave knowledge that it was the sculpture of the Hermes and no one was ever able to break it. The blue diamond which you were seeing on his head can buy half of our world. It was so strong that even a metal bends on hitting it and it was the only sculpture left in the whole world he ended. Everyone heard it with a great curiosity and left the place soon leaving Victor, Peter, Thomas and Johnson behind. Johnson who was still admiring the sculpture got a touch from someone and he looked back.

"So, is it precious?" asked Victor.

"Yes dear. Very precious", replied Johnson with a smiling face. Victor too smiled at him. Peter who also had some doubt came forward but Sebastian was in a hurry to report the Head boy. So he left that place.

Victor, Peter and the pot started admiring the sculpture and Thomas who is not at all interested in the sculpture was concentrating on some other area. Peter and Victor called out Thomas thrice but he was in his own world. Victor then went to Thomas and gave his shoulder a nudge. Thomas who smiled at his friends pointed something with his finger.

They saw a thin stick like figure with a red cloth on his head was running towards them. The boy has a very white glowing skin with a cute face. He came near the sculpture and looked at it with admiration then looked around.

At first he smiled at them and asked in a very polite way "Did they complete the explanation?"

Thomas who was curious stepped forward and said yes. His face grew little dull. On seeing this Thomas pointed out Peter and told the boy that Peter can explain it. He smiled and said "I don't think so"

Obviously Victor who didn't agree to the boy grew angry. Then the boy asked Peter "Ok. I will ask you a very simple question" saying this he went near the statue and pointed out the writing and asked "Do you know what Khunkhaar is?"

Peter who nodded his head asked "Do you know?"

The boy replied "The legend says that Khunkhaar is the name of the person who joins the two worlds and will be so powerful that even gods cannot beat him."

"Who is Khunkhaar then?" asked Peter with curiosity.

"Khunkhaar means a demon with a kind heart and we all know that no demon will be kind hearted so it was just a legend. That's the reason no can ever break it" he said. Just then there was a bell saying that the classes were about to start in five minutes.

When all these four turned backed and three were surprised to see that the hall was like an empty theater with no extra person. Victor who was already paying attention to his cutie pie cake was least bothered about his surroundings and the pot who was still feeling hungry was bothered about Victor so it jumped out of Peter's pocket and stood at the feet of Hermes where Victor was leaning and held his coat tight. It hung his coat to Hermes feet.

All started moving forward and Victor who didn't know about his situation took two steps ahead. By the second he realized he was going to fall he threw the cake and held Thomas collar tightly. The pot soon took the cake and flew into his master's pocket. Thomas in order to balance got hold of both Peter's and the new boy's hand.

Together all fell on the statue and it gave a huge thunder sound. All the students in the class room thought it as an earth quake and started yelling. The pot on other side started enjoying the feast.

The new boy who lifted his butt up first gave his hand to Thomas and Victor. All the three were shocked and terrible when they looked at Peter. Peter who didn't notice what has happened was happy to see that the statue didn't break.

"You crushed the stone" all the three shouted at once.

Peter who was still on the floor looked at his hands which are shining like thousands of diamonds placed at once and there were several pieces of diamond on the floor.

Soon all the students including Sebastian and Johnson was present at the hall. The hall was filled with noise of students.

All four friends looked at each other and held each other's hand tightly so that no one can separate them.

Sebastian who was furious asked loudly "Who did this?"

The room was then so much silent that the striking of the clock and landing of the feather can be heard. All the four dresses got bathed in the sweat and were shivering with fear but didn't let their hands go. Johnson's who liked them was feeling sorry for them.

Peter who felt that their friends shouldn't be blamed for his mistake comes forward facing the two heads before him.

Sebastian called out Johnson and told him to take Peter to decision box.

Peter was then blind folded because it was mandatory that no one should know the way and soon got vanished from the sight of his friends. He then turned many turnings with the head boy and finally reached an old room with two half and half doors. He was then asked by Johnson to stand on a large black metal plate with chains at his end. There was also a similar plate at the other side about 10 feet far from Peter.

Johnson opened a locker taking some leaves out of it. He entered something on a leaflet with a sharp needle like stick and made Peter to sign on it. The leaf says "Accused for breaking the sculpture". Peter signs and stands in the middle of the plate where Johnson had told to.

Peter was made to sit on that plate and then Johnson pressed a big red button on the other side wall of Peter. Within a fraction of seconds the large wall moved up leaving a place for a big stone to come towards the other side of the plate.

There in the hall Sebastian ordered the servants to retrieve the sculpture. Victor told his friends that they were lucky as nothing had happened to the sculpture and only the diamond was....

Victor was about to complete the sentence Thomas pointed his finger towards the sculpture. Victor and the new boy were now stepping their foot back noticing that the sculpture was already broken from inside and would fall down at any time.

The great sculpture had fallen down again and this time into pieces. Sebastian who was much more furious than before hold all the three students and taken them to balance just like Peter.

Peter who was curious and confused about what is happening around him noticed the stone. It was written 1 kg on it and was ten times the height of Peter. He was very much surprised to realize that it was a balance. John pulled the lever down which was beside him and Peter started to move up but didn't get balanced with the stone.

"It should balance actually. Why it is not balancing" John was talking to himself loud.

"That's because he is not alone in that" came Sebastian with all the three. He removed the folds and all friends are worried to see Peter at such a height.

"Is that..", "Is that..." Victor and Thomas were seeing their faces with astonishment.

"Yes" said the young boy, "It's a Hermes balance used in ancient times to measure the sins of a person."

"Looks like you are a bookworm. Then you must have also knew why it is not getting balanced" Said Sebastian crossing his arms.

"It doesn't balance it means that there are more people involved in it or the person may not be a sinner" said the boy.

"You are saying that we should be in there?" asked Victor with a crying face "I'm afraid of heights and I'm not going anywhere" said Victor stubbornly.

"Yes, we should be in there" said Thomas holding Victor's hand and dragged him to the plate. The plate came down with Peter in it and all joined him happily.

As the plate was moving upwards they are feeling terrible seeing the height. Victor then started to call out loudly "cupcakes.. cupcakes..cupcakes.."

All started staring at him. He explained that if he thinks about cupcakes he forgets about the height. They started laughing heart fully forgetting about the balance. The plate was still not balanced with the other one and it is true that no one had intentionally tried to destroy it.

The beast who was watching all the drama from the beginning had seen all the way and now it got reduced its size to small like an ant and dropped itself on the plate. Peter was able to sense it but couldn't do any as he was circled by his friends. He looked down for the signs of the beast and could not find any and everything is looking black in the plate.

The pot released both of its hands out and did some pushups and hand exercises to gain the strength then faced towards the plate and started pulling it downwards. It then slept without any disturbance.

Finally the Hermes balanced and there was a heavy blow of air and a leaf came out with a lighting of words "THE HERMES LIBRARY"

"So you have a detention of one week and you are going to work in the library of Hermes"

"Library of Hermes!" shouted all the three except Peter and sat down on the plate worried.

Johnson and Sebastian looked at each other surprised. John nodded his head as no and Sebastian sighed with his eyes that nothing would happen.

"No. You are not going to that library" said Sebastian with a deep thinking voice.

14

The Detention

Sebastian and Johnson talked for few minutes deciding not to send the boys to the LIBRARY. Later Johnson took all the boys blindfolded to the hall. All the four children stared at the sculpture as it was going into the store room forever. The sculpture which was once everything for the school was now thrown into the store room.

Johnson told us to wait near a portrait and added that Sebastian went to talk to the wise principal about the detention.

"Did Sebastian saw Principal?" asked Peter curiously. All become serious to listen to him.

"No" said Johnson laughing loudly, "Instead of thinking about the detention you people are thinking all this" he added.

"What is to worry about that library?" asked Peter calmly.

"What to worry! You should have seen your friends face when they heard about Hermes Library" said Johnson walking away from the boys and towards the stairs where Sebastian was supposed to come.

Peter then looked at the new boy for the answer.

"It was happened ages before when the gods used to live on the very place where we are now. It was said that THE LIBRARY was cursed by none other than Hermes himself. The Library was said to be magical and only a person can visit it in the day time and only for three times. Everyone knows the rule but it was said that something had happened between Hermes and his disciple. His disciple who was known for his obedience cheated Hermes and got inside in the night time for the blue stone" Said the new boy.

"Blue stone!" jumped Victor happily, "Is that the same stone which Peter had broken?"

"Yes but when the Hermes caught his disciple red handed with the stone he cursed it and also his disciple to stay like a stone. Now the stone doesn't possess any special powers and no one has ever seen it happened. It is also very dangerous to go into that library without possessing any special powers or skills" concluded the boy.

Now the bottom line is, "I don't want go into some stupid jungle and dead like no one" said the new boy.

"Wait! Did you say jungle?" asked Victor and Thomas.

"I thought you guys know" said the new boy drinking water.

Thomas and Victor face grew older like an old man. Soon Thomas recovered and started shooting the new boy with the questions.

"I am living nearby this city but still do not know much about it. How come you know much about it?" questioned Victor facing the new boy.

The new boy touched his red pagada with his hand and smiled at all the three. He told that his family got settled here for about 30years before and he was born and brought up here.

"So, what is your name?" asked Thomas with a smiling face.

"My name is Happy Singh" he said smiling, "What is your name?" he asked in return.

Thomas introduced himself and also his friends to the new boy and now they were looking for the Wise head of the school. Johnson then came hurried "Who all do not want to go to the forest?" he asked.

All raised their hands still holding their breath tightly looking at their friends' faces and waiting for the reply of Johnson. He then gave a piece of white paper to four of them and said that each of them owe him a chocolate for stopping their picnic to the jungle. All of them got relaxed after listening to him and asked what happened inside and what is with those white papers. He then explained that the principal thought for a while and said that they were given two options and to choose one.

"So what is the second option?" asked all at once.

"You have to attend Hermes next year for the schooling" said Johnson.

"What!" said Victor angrily "I have worked so much in the exam hall and we don't even know whether we will pass or not for the next year."

"Bravo! It means that you want to go to the forest?" asked Happy with his hands on waist.

"No" said Victor recovering soon "I meant if we have third option" he said slowly.

"This is the only option you have" said a strong voice from the back of them. All turned back as they already know that voice and there stands Sebastian crossing his hands. The beast that woke up listening to the Sebastian voice started looking out of Peter's pocket.

"Either you people go to the library or take rest for one year without coming to school" said Sebastian seriously and left the place. Johnson then told them to write and drop the papers in the box in front of them.

Having nothing to do with the situation all four wrote 'NO' as they don't want to go to the library and dropped the chits into the box and went to drink some water nearby.

The beast who was ready to give its best shot to torture Peter went back running into the box fast and decreased its size to small erasing all the 'NO'S' one after the other and replaced them with 'YES'. Johnson informed them to come to school next day and left the place taking the box to the principal.

All the four were happy about the forest but sad at the same time about Detention. Finally Happy Singh bid good bye to their friends and promised to meet them early the next day.

Peter, Victor and Thomas who reached orphanage did not want to share their sad story with Noby. So they kept their silence. Noby was walking fast with a joy in his face and held a basket in his hand. He came to their friends and opened the box and all were surprised to see color buttons.

"Holy Smoke!" said Victor "What are these?" Victor started jumping out of excitement like a monkey with dozens of banana. Noby and Thomas laughed at Victor's behavior. "Did Clovey send it?" He asked making his eyes big like a tortoise.

"These are vegetable cupcakes and yes Clovey brought it here. She came here to check my health" said Noby.

The pot in the Peter's pocket started scratching his leg for cupcakes. Peter kept two cupcakes into his pocket but pot didn't eat any. It was angry with the way Peter is throwing the cupcakes at it. It crossed its arms angrily and sat inside the pocket. It was happy though thinking that the real show would start at the school when they open the chits and its revenge will get fulfilled. It waited for some time but cannot stop the cupcakes coming into its stomach.

With the cupcakes coming in all forgot about the detention and ate heart fully and slept whole day.

It was eight in the evening and Thomas has already got ready. On seeing Thomas getting ready so soon, Victor and

Peter enquired about what is happening. He replied that happy Singh would be waiting for us in the school. Peter and Victor who remembered Singh jumped out of the bed and started to freshen up.

To reach HERMES which was 25kms long for them would take a vehicle. So they have waited for a vehicle to pass by. After two vehicles third vehicle gave them a lift.

The car was shabby black like a dried tree without any vibrant look. It got many cracks on it. None of them are willing to take the lift but remembering Happy Singh they got into the car. Victor and Thomas sat in the back seat while Peter accompanied the car owner at the front.

The car owner looked bore as that of his car and even worst. He didn't utter a single word in the journey. The children can't even see his face properly. He was all covered in black from top to bottom and was looking to them as if a shadow was driving the car.

Victor and Thomas who cannot shut their mouth more often stared showing their talent. Thomas told the owner about their orphanage and Victor gave the ending by narrating their urgency to the Hermes. The owner suddenly increased the speed and was driving fast. Thomas and Victor looked at each other horrified.

"Ugh! It's not that urgent uncle", said Thomas.

"Yes. You don't have to take any trouble for us uncle", said Victor.

That person was not listening to any of their wishes but driving rudely. Peter turned the wheel two to three times to avoid accident. There was a jewel box near the wheel of the car and all colored carved stones have fallen from the box due to his rash driving. Peter bent down and started collecting the stones. He looked at the brakes for a second and took all the stones into the box. The owner speed is now going off the limits.

"Is there any shortcut from this forest to reach Hermes", asked Thomas hurriedly pointing his hand outside of the window towards the forest to the owner. The owner then stopped the car and pointed out a dark forest with a narrow path in it.

All the three held their pants tight so that they don't get wet and jumped out of the car as soon as possible. Thomas and Victor started hopping into the forest and were neither bothered about the darkness of the forest nor about Peter who was stilling facing the owner to return a carved stone which got on his shirt.

Peter returned the stone to the owner and started walking slowly in his friends' path. Suddenly he turned back as he remembered something. To his astonishment there was no sign of the car and the owner till the end of the long road. There were even no sideways in the forest to take turning. All these thoughts are running in his mind. Peter then unconsciously started walking fast and crossed their friends.

He remembered that when he picked the stones he looked at the brakes and there was no feet of that owner and also he remembered when he returned the stone on the owner's glove hands it gave a sound as if it had fallen inside the car crossing the body of the owner. Peter is now terrified and was sweating a lot. Thomas and Victor accompanied Peter and enquired him about his terrible face.

"Run as fast as possible. We shouldn't be here" said Peter in a strong tone.

"How can we go so fast without any light?",growled Victor " We only have moonlight here" he then added.

Thomas got something in his mind and he ran quickly towards the shy plants nearby and made a cone out of it. He then started making sounds with it. Soon several light buzz insects gathered them showing light. They walked as fast as they can and soon reached a wooden log in front of them and also a carved stone few yards away from the log. The carved stone was carved with the symbol → and there were bold letters " HERMES ……" was written vertically and also there was some other word under Hermes which was hidden with stones and there was lots of clay on it.

"I can see our school bell tower from here. If we cross this path and go fast then maybe we can reach there", Said Thomas. All agreed. As soon as they crossed the log they turned back because all the three felt that they have crossed the border of their world and reached some other world.

All looked at each other. They also realized that the buzz bees are no more following them. Now they have to rely on moonlight to forward their journey. Suddenly there was a huge earthquake and the log rolled down the way the children had come.

They somehow made themselves up, dusted their already dusted pants and were looking forward for their way out. The climate was already worst with huge thunders and the wind. They didn't know that there was some surprise waiting right in front of them. They have no idea that they unknowingly reached the place where they never want to go even in their dreams.

They stood in front of that mighty carved stone planning which way would be easy to reach school early. Just then there was a huge lightening on the carved stone and all the small stones which covered the down part of the carved stone rubbed the dry clay down showing them their worst nightmare.

"THE H E R M E S L I B R A R Y"

It was sculptured on it with huge patterns

All three were frozed like an ice, also forgot for few seconds that they were humans and can speak. They started sighing to one another. Finally Victor broke the silent talk.

"What?" shouted Victor at the top of his voice.

"Run!" shouted Victor and Peter.

All started running at different routes away from the Hermes library statue. They finally reached the central part and were few miles away from the school.

Just then they saw that the grasses are shaking with a heavy speed. Victor and Thomas were standing still and Peter who was curious moved his foot two steps forward.

A vehicle with thundering storm jumped out of the grass from the top of Peter's head crossing Victor and Thomas. A figure jumped out of the vehicle and moved forward to attack them.

Not knowing what to do, Peter started running for his life. There were few more cars which appeared from other directions finally rounded Peter. Now he is helpless.

The beast inside his pocket was sleeping happily without any problem. It was not bothered about anything happening in its surroundings. The cars then started to horn so loudly and Peter closed his ears. He fell ill and knelt down to reduce that unpleasant sound.

All the cars started to come close to Peter continuing the horn sound. The beast who got irritated by the sound just woke up from its legendary sleep. It came out from his pocket and did some neck exercises and pushups, then washed its face with the water nearby.

Beast hates when someone wakes it up. It attacked all cars one by one and they got transformed into humans. All of them looked like dry branches of the tree and had masks on their face hiding their identification and they did not have any shadows. Peter identified one hoodie among who attacked him last time. That hoodie has different appearance when compared to other hoodies. His hoodie was designed with a mysterious kind of tree on his back.

After transformation they started attacking Peter again but he looked at the beast smiling. The beast nodded its head that it won't help. Peter himself tried to protect from them. All were of same height of Peter but the only difference they have was they are trained for any kind of circumstances. They started shooting arrows from their hands and now their body looked blacker than before.

     PETER AND THE MAGICAL POT

Peter failed after trying to protect him several times. He showed beast the head plate of it. Beast was angry with Peter's behavior. Anyway it again started attacking all of them. It stroked everyone all fell down at a time. Knowing that they cannot protect themselves anymore, they started protecting their head like a shield. Now their hands are looking like dry trees branches.

Pot attacked the shield with such a speed that all got scattered and turned into empty. There was a huge hit on the tree hoodie's hand and he has fallen down.

Peter said Thank you to pot and requested it get inside the pocket. The beast was not ready to go because it was hurt by Peter's behavior. He then showed it a cupcake and finally made it sleep inside the pocket. He heard someone running towards him at the back. He turned suddenly that the hoodie woke up.

He got hit by Thomas and they fall down. Peter then narrated the whole story eliminating Beast from all the scenes. The beast who woke up by this hit wanted to smash Peter with hammer for eliminating its heroism. Thomas and Peter went near the hoodie slowly and they have removed the hood.

Peter and Thomas looked at each other in surprise.

"Cecilia!" said Thomas in a cold voice.

She was lying on the land with bruises on her body. Suddenly she opened her eyes and pushed Thomas hard with her hand on his chest. Thomas went like a flash and hit a tree which is in the slope of a valley. Thomas held the tree tightly but slipped and dropped down into a valley where he held a small branch which was taking weight of Thomas on one side and lifting the other side. Thomas started shouting out of his mouth.

Peter ran towards Thomas while the pot jumped from his pocket to protect them from Cecilia. First he had fallen on his knees then his whole body toughed the ground when he held Thomas hand tight and lost his grip. He then landed on the other side of the branch accompanying Thomas. Thomas thanked Peter for making a balance.

The pot on other hand started attacking Cecilia. Both had strokes on each other. Hoodie got much affected by the attack, she ran off into the brightness. Soon the darkness took its place again. Pot's hand got hurt a little. It needs food to cure itself.

Victor who became conscious runs to them when he heard them shout and pulled them up with the help of a climber. While Victor taking to the Thomas about the situation Peter took pot into his pocket.

All of them reached the gate where Happy Singh was waiting for him. He was roaming here and there not knowing what to know. He then saw his friends and ran to them to tell something important but seeing them in that kind of situation he first decided to let them treat.

Happy Singh is basically very calm but today his behavior is kind of different thought Thomas in his mind. All were treated well in the nursing home. Peter took some cotton to wash room and tied band to pot's hand. The pot was about to ask for food but his friends called him out so Peter rushed out.

"What happened to you guys?" asked Happy Singh rising up.

"Well, I think you don't want to hear about it" said Victor looking at Thomas and Peter.

On insisting Thomas narrated the whole story to Happy. He also told how bravely Peter faced Cecilia and others.